Drone
Detective

written by Mari Kesselring
illustrated by Mariano Epelbaum

This book is a PRIZE from
DRAYTON VALLEY LIBRARIES
PH: 780-514-2722 / 780-514-3800

12 STORY LIBRARY

www.12StoryLibrary.com

Copyright © 2015 by Peterson Publishing Company, North Mankato, MN 56003. All rights reserved. No part of this book may be reproduced or utilized in any form or by any means without written permission from the publisher.

12-Story Library is an imprint of Peterson Publishing Company and Press Room Editions.

Produced for 12-Story Library by Red Line Editorial

Illustrations by Mariano Epelbaum

ISBN
978-1-63235-041-1 (hardcover)
978-1-63235-101-2 (paperback)
978-1-62143-082-7 (hosted ebook)

Library of Congress Control Number: 2014946004

Printed in the United States of America
Mankato, MN
October, 2014

Table of Contents

1

A Group of Three

The new message alert went off on Bridget's smartphone. Even though she was running late, she couldn't resist checking it. Kids at Blue Lake Junior High were allowed to use their phones during school but only between classes and at lunch.

Check this out, Trevor had written her. He included a link to a website in his message. Trevor was president of Blue Lake's Tech Club, and since Bridget was probably the most tech-obsessed 12-year-old in the universe, he always sent her links to tech stuff.

Bridget glanced at the time. She had a minute to spare before her third-period science class, so she opened the link.

"Regional Technology in Science Fair," read the website's headline. Bridget skimmed the text with interest. Junior high and high school students were invited to submit science projects that involved using technology to study an environmental topic. The prize for first place was $2,000. Bridget's heart beat faster thinking of all the cool gadgets and apps she could buy with that money. And she was seriously low on cash after upgrading her smartphone last month.

As she ducked into her classroom, Bridget read that Margaret Knutson would be judging the contest. Dr. Knutson was a technology scientist who had developed special tracking collars for endangered wolves. Bridget had read about her work on several social networking sites.

$2,000 and a chance to meet Dr. Knutson! Bridget thought, taking her seat. *I have to enter.*

"Please take out your tablets and look at chapter seven," Ms. Diaz, Bridget's science teacher, said as she breezed into the room.

Bridget put her phone in her backpack. She'd check out how to enter the contest later.

"We're going to start our final group research project today," Ms. Diaz explained.

Project?! Bridget perked up. This might give her a perfect opportunity to enter the Technology in Science Fair.

Plus, I've already got my group partners picked out, Bridget thought, glancing over at her friends Eric and Emma.

Third-period science class was probably the best part of Bridget's day. It was the only class that she, Emma, and Eric were all in together. Emma had been Bridget's best friend forever, and Eric lived next door to her. Better yet, Eric and Emma usually got along with each other.

Ms. Diaz had assigned seats, so Bridget didn't sit next to Eric or Emma during class. But they often worked on group projects and studied for tests together.

Ms. Diaz was showing the pages from chapter 7 on the classroom's Smart Board. Bridget sat up a little straighter in her seat as she pulled up the chapter on her own tablet computer. Because Bridget loved all things tech, she found it easier to pay attention in class if her teachers used technology too.

Bridget's whole life revolved around technology. Her father was Nick Grant, president of Lingo, a technology company in Cyber Hills, and Bridget had access to a lot of cutting-edge gadgets. It was the reason why almost everyone in school, except for the teachers, called her Bridget Gadget.

"The purpose of this project is to hone your scientific observation skills," Ms. Diaz explained. "You'll want to pick a topic to observe over a two-week period. It can be anything—animals, plants, stars. You just need to present a reason for picking your subject."

Bridget smiled when she saw Emma raise her hand. She already knew what Emma was going to ask.

"Yes, Emma?" Ms. Diaz said.

"Can we pick our own groups for the project?"

Ms. Diaz nodded. "Yes, you can."

Emma smiled over her shoulder at Bridget, and Bridget nodded towards Eric on the left side of the room. Their group was set.

"In fact, let's pick groups now," Ms. Diaz said. "Gather with your partners and then I'll explain this more."

Bridget sprang from her chair and headed toward Emma. She waved at Eric to follow her over, but he was already on his way.

Bridget and Eric pulled up chairs by Emma's table.

"You guys got here fast," Emma joked.

Ms. Diaz looked around the room.

"Okay, so we have one group of two," Ms. Diaz said, looking at Grant Jung and Ella Reynolds, who sat so close to each other that Bridget had to look twice to make sure they were sitting on separate chairs.

Grant and Ella were dating. They held hands at lunch and in the hallway. Every time Bridget saw them, she couldn't help but feel a little weird about it. She'd heard that some kids in the sixth grade were already dating. Bridget had a crush or two herself, but she didn't think she was ready to date. Besides, she doubted her dad would even allow it. She was glad none of her friends were dating either.

"Okay, I guess it's okay to have one group of two," Ms. Diaz said after a moment.

Ms. Diaz let the groups brainstorm what they would like to observe for the project.

"What about the foxes in Williams Park?" Emma said after a minute. "I've seen them in my backyard, and it'd be fun to learn how they survive next to an urban area."

Bridget squinted at Emma, mulling over her idea. How could she connect fox observations to technology so they could enter their project in the Technology in Science Fair?

"Sounds great," Eric said. "But aren't foxes scared of people? Will we be able to get close enough to observe them?"

"They usually run away if they see me," Emma said.

"Wait," Bridget said as a spark of a thought entered her mind. "Maybe there's another way to observe the foxes—"

"Like setting up a hidden camera?" Emma asked.

Bridget nodded slowly. "Yeah . . . or maybe using a drone."

2

Robotic Research

"A drone?" Emma's eyes widened. "Really?"

Bridget nodded. A drone would be perfect, and several tech companies had created research drones. Using a drone would also qualify their project for the Technology in Science Fair.

"A drone with a camera to observe foxes . . ." Eric said thoughtfully. "Do you actually have anything like that, Gadget?"

"Well, no," Bridget admitted. "But let me check with my dad. I thought Lingo developed some sort of drone a couple years ago. And just think about it. We could get video footage of the foxes in their actual habitat, not just in Emma's backyard. It would be amazing!"

"Plus, if we use a drone for our project, we could enter this contest," Bridget added. She told them all about the Technology in Science Fair she'd learned about from Trevor.

Eric's eyes widened at the mention of the prize money. "Whoa, $2,000? Cool!"

"Sounds like a great idea," Emma agreed. "Can you talk to your dad tonight?"

Bridget nodded. "No problem."

"Then I'll do some research on foxes to learn about their habits," Eric offered.

"And I'll explore the park for signs of foxes," Emma said excitedly.

That night, Bridget had to wait until 9:00 for her dad to get home from work. Sometimes he worked really long days, especially when he was in the middle of an important project.

"Hey, Dad!" Bridget said as she gave him a hug at the door.

"Hi, Bridg! How was your day?"

Bridget didn't even wait for her dad to set down his briefcase before she launched into the description of her science project, and her desperate need to use a Lingo drone.

"We want to observe foxes, like what they eat and how they behave. But they are scared of people, so we were thinking a drone would really be our best option," Bridget explained excitedly.

Bridget's dad smiled at her enthusiasm. "Your timing couldn't be better," he said, holding out his smartphone. On the screen was an article with the headline, "Lingo Introduces Silent Research Drone."

Bridget quickly scanned the article. The drone had been developed for researchers who were concerned about disturbing wildlife during their fieldwork. It was exactly what Bridget needed for her research project.

"It's been in development for a long time," Bridget's dad explained. "But it was officially released to the market today."

"Do you think I could use one for our project?" Bridget asked hopefully.

"I think so," her dad responded thoughtfully. "The government has placed restrictions on the use of drones because they can be harmful to wildlife. Lingo requires companies to submit a research proposal before purchasing one of its drones. So you, Eric, and Emma will need to do the same."

"I can do that! No problem," Bridget said.

"If you get it to me tomorrow," her dad said, "I'll fast track it so you have it in time for your project."

"Great!" Bridget squealed.

Bridget quickly texted Eric and Emma, *Lingo has a silent drone.*

Silent? Eric wrote back.

So they don't disturb the wildlife.

Cool, Emma texted.

Bridget was super excited. With a drone as part of their project, they'd win first prize at the Technology in Science Fair, and she'd get to meet Dr. Knutson for sure.

3

Driving the Drone

A few days later, Bridget's dad walked
into the house holding a large box
with a Lingo logo stamped on the side.

"Well, I have some good news," Bridget's
dad announced.

"Wow," Bridget breathed. "The drone!"

"Everyone at Lingo was supportive of
you using a drone for your school project,"
Bridget's dad explained. "You know, we always
try to support educational endeavors."

Bridget usually rolled her eyes when her
dad started talking about Lingo's business
practices, but she was so excited about the
drone that she barely heard him.

"We need to download the drone
controller app onto your phone so that you'll
be able to control the drone and see what its

camera is picking up," Bridget's dad explained. "Lingo has granted you one license for usage."

"That's okay," Bridget said. "I'll just share my phone with Eric and Emma."

Bridget's dad smiled as he slowly lifted the drone out of the box and set it on the kitchen table. Bridget had never seen a drone up close before. She'd only heard about them

on the news and in videos she'd watched online. Not much larger than a basketball, Lingo's drone was white with the Lingo logo on the top. Four bars reached out from the body of the drone. At the end of each arm were small propellers like those on a helicopter.

"You know you need to be very careful with this, okay?" Bridget's dad said. "It's not like your phone or your tablet. This drone is for your research project *only*. It's part of Lingo's education and research initiative."

"Yeah, dad." Bridget rolled her eyes. Couldn't he once give her a piece of tech without some type of lecture attached to it? "I know. I'll be careful."

He sighed. "I know. Just a reminder. Let's download the app onto your phone, and I'll show you how to work it."

"Okay!" Bridget hopped a little in her excitement.

Bridget and her dad took the drone for its first flight. Their backyard was pretty open, so she didn't have to worry about many obstacles, and controlling the drone came naturally to her.

"Looks like you're getting the hang of it!" Bridget's dad said with obvious pride during Bridget's third test flight.

Bridget carefully landed the drone on the grass in front of her and then snapped a photo of it with her smartphone to send to Emma and Eric.

Let's start our project! Emma's house in an hour? Bridget texted.

Whoa! Come on over! Emma texted back immediately.

On my way, Eric texted.

Within half an hour, the three group members were gathered in Emma's backyard, ready to launch the drone into Williams Park for their first fox observation.

"You guys ready?" Bridget asked as she pulled up the drone app on her phone.

"Totally," Emma said. "Let 'er fly!"

"You know how to steer it, right?" Eric said, looking worried. "Like, you've practiced?"

Bridget sighed. Eric could be such a worrier.

"Yeah, I practiced with my dad in our backyard. Stop worrying."

"I'm just asking . . ."

"Okay, stand back a little," Bridget instructed as she switched the drone's power switch to the on position. They all stepped back from the drone as Bridget used the app on her phone to start the drone's propellers spinning. Slowly it lifted off the ground.

"Whoa . . ." Emma breathed, watching the drone fly up around the trees.

Bridget smiled proudly and pointed to the screen on her phone. "Look, the camera shows where the drone is pointing."

"There's a clearing behind this row of trees with some hollowed-out tree trunks around the edge of the forest. I read foxes like to sleep in dens like that."

"Let's check if they're there!" Bridget said as she aimed the drone where Emma directed.

"So, I don't mean to be negative," Eric said slowly, "but the research I've done says we're not very likely to see a fox during the day. They usually come out in the evening and sleep during the day."

"But it's worth a try, right?" Bridget said. Flying the drone was so much fun, she didn't want to stop.

"Well, I guess it doesn't hurt," Eric said.

After an hour of searching, they hadn't seen a single fox.

"I don't think this is going to be as easy as we thought," Emma finally said.

But Bridget wasn't about to give up. "Let's keep trying!"

Eric glanced at the clock on his phone. "I've gotta get home for dinner. My dad's making pot roast."

Bridget sighed impatiently. "All right, but let's meet back here at dusk tonight."

"Okay," Eric said, but Bridget could tell he was thinking more about pot roast and less about foxes.

As if on cue, Emma's mom yelled from the porch. "Emma! Dinner!"

"Guess I've gotta go too," Emma said.

"Okay," Bridget said. "See you guys both back here in about an hour." Bridget used her phone app to steer the drone out of the woods. She watched it emerge from between the trees. As the drone approached, aiming its camera at them, Bridget could see herself, Eric, and Emma on the screen of her smartphone. Bridget guided the drone safely to the ground and picked it up.

"One hour," Bridget said. "See you soon."

Back at her own house, Bridget was disappointed to find that her dad wasn't home. He had left a plate of chicken and rice for her in the refrigerator. Not pot roast, but it wasn't bad either.

Bridget decided to look up the details of the Technology in Science Fair to pass the time. Bridget pulled her laptop onto her lap as she sat down on the couch. She scrolled through the contest page and clicked "Submission Guidelines."

Immediately, Bridget's heart dropped into her stomach. The first requirement for participating in the contest was listed at the top of the page: "Each contest submission requires a $50 entry fee."

Fifty bucks? Bridget couldn't believe it. She didn't have fifty dollars. In fact, she had *zero* dollars.

Bridget texted Emma and Eric, *Do u guys have $50?*

Emma texted back, *No why?*

Excuse me? Eric texted.

Bridget rolled her eyes. They were due to meet back at Emma's anyway, so Bridget raced out the door and shivered in the chill of a spring evening. She felt defeated. Bridget had used up every last cent of her allowance from the past several months to upgrade her phone. Plus her dad had even agreed to loan her some money to cover the cost. She was broke.

4

Money Woes

"Fifty dollars?" Eric half shouted. They were standing in Emma's backyard again. The sky was getting dark, and they needed to get moving, but first Bridget had filled them in on the entry fee for the contest.

"Fifty bucks to enter a lousy contest?" Eric repeated, still shocked.

"So neither of you have fifty dollars to spare?" Bridget asked solemnly.

Emma shook her head no.

Eric raised his eyebrows. "The best I could do is scrounge up some change off my bedroom floor."

Bridget sighed. "I really want to enter," she said, thinking about Dr. Knutson and all the amazing things she'd accomplished with technology. It would be a dream fulfilled to actually meet her. Bridget hoped they'd find a way to get the money.

"Well, let's get started," Emma said. "If we never see any foxes, we won't have anything worth submitting to the contest, not to mention getting a big fat zero on our science project."

"You're right," Eric said. "Bridget, want to fire up that drone?"

Bridget shrugged halfheartedly and turned on the device.

"I hope we'll be able to see something," Emma said. "It's getting dark."

"Any lights on that thing?" Eric asked.

"Nope," Bridget said. "The foxes might freak out if we shined a spotlight at them."

"Yeah, I suppose," Eric laughed.

Bridget watched the screen on her phone as she guided the drone over the trees and into a clearing in the middle of the park.

"Maybe they'll be out here hunting rabbits or something," Bridget said.

"I hope so," Eric said as they crowded around Bridget's phone. "Otherwise—"

"Oh my gosh!" Bridget whispered. "Look!"

On the screen, a small brownish-red animal trotted through some tall grasses. Bridget pressed the record button on the app to save the footage.

"Is that a fox or . . . a raccoon?" Eric questioned.

Bridget zoomed in on the animal.

"A fox!" Emma exclaimed. She had pulled up a photo of a fox on her smartphone and was comparing it to the animal on Bridget's screen.

"This is way cool," Bridget said, finally smiling again. "We did it!"

The next morning, Bridget had a text from Emma.

What bout asking Diaz 4 $50? Like from the school? Emma's text read.

Bridget perked up immediately. Ms. Diaz was really involved with her students. She ran the science club on Tuesdays after school. She'd probably be excited to hear that their group wanted to enter the contest.

Yea! I will! Bridget texted back. *Thx!*

Later that day, Bridget rushed into her science class a few minutes early. She wrinkled her nose when she saw that Grant and Ella were already in the classroom. They snuggled as close to each other as possible. *Gross.*

Ms. Diaz sat at the front of the classroom, looking at something on her computer, probably trying to ignore the lovebirds.

"Ms. Diaz!" Bridget called as she made a beeline toward her teacher.

"Bridget, what can I help you with? How's the project going?"

Eager for an answer, Bridget quickly explained the guidelines for the science fair. "Would the school pay for the entry fee?"

"Well," Ms. Diaz frowned. "If we enter your group in the contest, then we'd need to enter all the other groups. It's only fair. And unfortunately, the school doesn't have the budget for that."

"Oh, okay," Bridget said, trying to hide the disappointment in her voice.

"But there are contests that don't have entry fees at all," Ms. Diaz said. "I can get you a listing of some of the most popular ones."

"Do you think Dr. Knutson is judging any of those contests?" Bridget asked.

Ms. Diaz smiled knowingly. "I don't think so. But they might still be very worthwhile."

"Okay," Bridget said. She dragged herself back to her seat and plopped down in her chair. Meeting Margaret Knutson was really impossible now.

She texted Emma, *No luck w/ Diaz.*

When Emma walked into the classroom, she already had her "concerned best friend" expression on her face.

"Bummer, Gadg," Emma said. "But at least the project is going well!"

"Thanks, Emma," Bridget said.

"Okay, class," Ms. Diaz said from the front of room. "Let's meet with our group members quickly to check in."

Bridget and Eric headed over to Emma's table. Ms. Diaz had each group report to the class about their progress. It was pretty interesting. Some kids were observing wildflowers. One group was watching the stars and planets in the night sky. Another group was researching bees.

As the class period came to an end, Bridget thought they should make a plan for when they would next observe the foxes.

"How about tonight?" Bridget threw out.

"Sure," Eric said. "We should meet *after* dinner this time."

"Sounds good to me," Emma said.

The bell rang and the three friends gathered up their books. Bridget was the first one to the door. She paused to wait for Emma. They both had P.E. next.

"Go ahead, Gadg," Emma said. "I need to ask Eric about our history homework."

"You do?" Eric asked, puzzled.

"Yeah, remember?" Emma gave Eric a goofy smile that Bridget had never seen before.

"Oh, okay," Bridget said, walking out of the classroom with a confused look on her face.

5

Secrets

That evening, Bridget texted Eric,
Wanna walk 2 Emma's 2gether?

Because Bridget and Eric were next-door
neighbors, they often walked places together.

Already at the park, he texted back.

k, c u there, Bridget responded.

"Were you playing basketball?" Bridget
asked Eric when she arrived at Emma's
house. Eric liked to shoot hoops at the park
sometimes.

"Basketball? Uh, no," Eric said.

"What were you doing at the park, then?"
Bridget asked, curious.

"The park? Oh, right. Nothing really." Eric's
face started to get red. "Just hanging out."

Emma came out of her house through the back porch. Her dog, Abby, ran out after her. A small brown mass of shaggy fur, Abby dashed around the yard yipping at Bridget.

"Abby!" Bridget exclaimed, kneeling down.

Abby just kept barking.

"Shh!" Emma hissed at Abby. "You'll scare the foxes away."

Eric reached down and picked the dog up. He rubbed her ears to calm her down. Abby's shaggy tail wagged back and forth.

"Whoa," Bridget said as she watched Eric. "Are you like the dog whisperer? Abby hates people she doesn't really know."

"Uh," Eric said, turning red again. "I guess she just likes me."

Bridget turned to Emma, but her friend just shrugged and avoided eye contact.

"I'll put her inside," Emma suggested, gathering Abby from Eric's arms.

As Emma walked back up the porch with Abby, Bridget turned to Eric.

"Okay, why are you being weird?"

"Weird?" Eric squeaked. "I'm being weird?"

Bridget felt like Eric was hiding something, but before she could question him further, Emma came back.

"Let's find some foxes!" Emma said with urgency. "It's getting dark!"

Bridget fired up the drone and flew it into the meadow. It wasn't long before Bridget spotted a flash of reddish-brown fur.

"Whoa!" Eric said, leaning over Bridget's shoulder. "It's moving fast."

"Something scared it," Emma said, frowning.

"Wait, where's it going?" Bridget's mouth hung open as the three of them watched the fox crawl and leap its way up into the branches of a tree.

"It climbed up a tree," Emma gasped.

"Yeah! I read that they do that sometimes when they are scared," Eric said. "I can't believe we got it on video!"

"Awesome!" Bridget said, smiling. "Wait! Is that another one?" Bridget saw the glow of eyes in the brush near the bottom of the tree.

"Wow! Two foxes!" Emma yelped.

In the excitement, Bridget had forgotten about the weirdness between her friends, but then Eric turned to Emma and said, "Probably would've seen three foxes if it wasn't for your crazy mutt."

And Emma, who usually ignored Eric's jokes, playfully punched his shoulder.

Weird, Bridget thought. *They seem a little friendlier than usual.*

Bridget woke up the next morning, thankful that it was Saturday. She hadn't slept well and was still confused over her friends' behavior last night. Today they had planned to meet at Emma's around 2:00 for one last flight with the drone and to review the footage they already had. Their project was due Monday. Monday also happened to be the deadline for applying to the Technology in Science Fair.

But Bridget tried hard not to think too much about that.

Bridget decided to hang out at the Cyber Hills Web Café and review some of the drone footage before meeting up with her friends. It was the only place open this early on Saturday and within biking distance of Bridget's house.

At the café, Bridget sat down at a table with a mocha and her laptop. Just then, the door swung open. Grant and Ella strolled in, holding hands, of course.

Great, Bridget thought. *How am I supposed to get any work done with them getting cozy?*

They settled down at a table on the opposite side of the room. Clearly, this was a date. Bridget tried to focus on her work, but something else nagged at her.

What if Eric and Emma were secretly *dating*? It was too crazy to be true, and yet the more Bridget thought about it, the more it seemed to make sense. Recently they'd been friendlier with each other than ever before.

This is a disaster, Bridget thought to herself. If Eric and Emma were dating, that made Bridget the third wheel. Bridget felt sure that pretty soon they'd be ditching her so that they could hang out as a couple. Maybe they already had!

Besides that, Bridget felt shocked that her friends felt ready to date. Bridget and Emma talked all the time about who they thought was cute or who they were crushing on. But Emma had never mentioned actually wanting to date someone. Bridget frowned. Was Emma growing up without her?

Bridget took a deep breath.

Chill out, she told herself. *You don't even know if they are really dating*, she thought. *Not for sure.*

Bridget had just managed to calm herself down when another thought entered her mind, making her upset all over again.

If they are dating, why are they keeping it secret from me?

Bridget knew that Eric's parents didn't want him to date until high school, but why wouldn't he trust Bridget with this secret? She'd always been a loyal friend to him. Then there was Emma. Bridget had thought that she and Emma kept zero secrets. Since they were little, they'd told each other everything. Emma was the only person who knew that Bridget still slept with her favorite stuffed animal, Cyber the cat. And Bridget was pretty sure she was the only person who knew Emma had accidentally stolen a candy bar in second grade by simply walking out of a drugstore with it in her hand.

Bridget always imagined that Emma would tell her everything about her first boyfriend, even if it *was* Eric.

How could she not tell me? Bridget thought.

Bridget pressed her palms against her forehead. This was crazy. She *had* to know what was going on. Were they really dating?

Bridget took out her smartphone and texted Emma, *If u were dating someone, u'd tell me. Right?*

Bridget anxiously peered at the protective covering on her smartphone screen as she waited for a reply. Nothing. Emma, like Bridget, usually responded to texts right away.

Bridget couldn't keep the thoughts from rushing into her mind. *What if Eric and Emma are together right now?* she thought. *On a date just like Grant and Ella?*

Bridget texted Eric, *Wanna play b-ball?*

Eric loved basketball and was always bugging Bridget to play. If he saw the text, he'd respond right away . . . unless he was on a date.

Bridget waited for several minutes, staring at her smartphone screen in the hope that it would light up with a message. Again, nothing.

6

Tracking the Truth

An hour later, there were still no messages from Eric or Emma. Bridget squirmed in her chair at the Cyber Hills Web Café, trying to distract herself by reviewing the fox footage. She nearly jumped out of her skin when her phone vibrated with a text message from Eric.

No time 4 b-ball 2day. Sry!

Bridget had just caught her breath when another text startled her again. This one was from Emma.

Of course I would! Why?

Bridget shook her head. *This proves it,* she thought. *They must've been hanging out together. Why else would they respond at the exact same time?*

Bridget stared at her phone blankly. How could they keep this from her? Bridget couldn't remember the last time she'd felt this low. But it was almost 2:00. She had to go to Emma's.

When Bridget arrived at Emma's, Eric and Emma were already in the backyard and sitting in the grass.

I wonder how their date went, Bridget thought bitterly.

"Hey, Gadg!" Emma called out cheerfully when she saw Bridget approach.

"Ready for our final flight?" Eric asked.

"Yeah, I guess," Bridget muttered, avoiding eye contact. She wondered if she should just come right out and say it: *I know you're dating.* But she didn't have any concrete proof, so they'd probably just deny it, just as Emma already had in her text message. It was no use.

"You sleep okay?" Emma asked, looking concerned. "You seem crabby."

"Whatever," Bridget snapped. "Let's just get this over with."

"Uh . . . okay," Emma said. Eric shifted uncomfortably from foot to foot.

The final observation yielded no results. Bridget did a sloppy job of flying the drone and almost crashed it into a tree more than once. She just didn't care much about the project at that moment.

"Oh well," Eric said when they were done. "We got footage of a fox climbing a tree. There was no way we were gonna beat that anyway. I think the project will turn out okay."

"Me too!" Emma said. "Should we meet tomorrow to write up the report of our findings?"

"Yeah, sure," Bridget mumbled, focusing on packing up the drone.

"Sounds like a plan," Eric said.

Bridget tucked the drone under her arm and turned to Emma. "See you then," she said.

"Are you okay?" Emma asked. "You're acting weird."

"*I'm* acting weird?" Bridget snapped. *Unbelievable.* "Whatever."

Emma stepped back, looking hurt.

"Eric," Bridget demanded, turning to her friend, "are you walking home with me?"

Eric looked nervous. *Really* nervous. "Uh, actually Gadget, Emma was gonna help me with some history homework. Catch you later?"

"Fine," Bridget said. She hurried away before her friends could see the tears welling up in her eyes.

History homework? Yeah, right! Bridget thought as she furiously tore across Emma's yard and onto the sidewalk. She couldn't believe her best friends would continue to lie to her face. Was she just supposed to keep pretending she was clueless?

Bridget ducked behind some hedges in Emma's neighbor's front yard. Lots of kids from school lived in Emma's neighborhood. Bridget didn't really want anyone to see her crying.

She wiped her eyes with the back of her hand and tried to get a hold of her emotions— it wasn't easy.

Just then, Bridget heard a familiar voice calling out.

"Wait up, Emma!"

It was Eric. Bridget was sure of it. Bridget peeked through the hedge just in time to see Emma and Eric whiz by on their bikes.

Bridget's heart started to pound. She'd been right all along. And now, Bridget eyed the drone she was still holding.

Bridget *knew* she was only supposed to use the drone for her school project. She *knew* it wasn't a toy. And she *knew* that her dad would be furious if she used it for anything other than her project.

But in that moment, Bridget wanted the truth. She was sick of feeling like she was being lied to. Bridget set the drone on the grass in front of her. She opened her drone controller app and steered the drone up over the hedges in pursuit of her two friends on their bikes.

7

Surveillance Shock

Bridget carefully steered the drone after Eric and Emma as they rode down the street on their bikes. Bridget kept the drone high in the sky and behind her friends so they wouldn't be likely to see it.

Bridget didn't have to follow Eric and Emma for very long. They stopped their bikes in front of a small blue house just two blocks from Emma's house. Eric walked up to the front door and knocked. Someone—Bridget couldn't see who through the leaves of a tree in the front yard—opened the door. Then, the home's garage door opened, and Emma and Eric both went inside the garage.

What is going on? Bridget thought. *Whose house is this?*

The garage door remained open, and Bridget could see movement inside the garage. But it was difficult to see what was going on from the angle of the drone's camera.

Bridget watched as Emma pulled a trash can out onto the driveway and then went back into the garage.

What are they doing?

Bridget took a deep breath. She had to get a closer look. Bridget lowered the drone, getting a peek into the garage. *Was Eric holding a broom?*

Bridget saw the front door of the house open again. A woman walked out of the house holding two glasses of water on a tray. She headed toward the garage. Bridget zoomed the drone's camera in on the woman's face. She nearly yelped in surprise. She recognized the woman.

It was Ms. Diaz!

What on earth are Emma and Eric doing at Ms. Diaz's house?

Ms. Diaz handed the drinks to Emma, and then went back inside the house.

Just as Bridget started to zoom out the camera, she saw a mass of green leaves and brown branches on the screen. The image on her screen swirled violently. The drone was spinning out of control. She caught glimpses of the roof of the house, the tree, the pavement of the driveway, and the lawn as the drone spun out of control. Desperately, Bridget used the controls to try to pull the drone back up and out of the tree, but it was too late. Bridget saw the green grass of the lawn before the screen went dark.

8

Ground Control

The second the screen on her drone controller app went dark, Bridget jumped up from behind the hedges and raced toward the blue house. If the drone was broken, she was going to be in *huge* trouble.

As she ran, Bridget tried to piece things together. It made no sense. Emma and Eric were hanging out with Ms. Diaz. Why?

When Bridget made it to the little blue house, she wasn't surprised to see Emma and Eric hunched over the drone, which had crashed in the middle of the yard. Luckily, nothing on the outside looked damaged. But the screen had gone blank, so maybe the technology inside or the camera had been damaged.

"Bridget!" Emma exclaimed when she saw her. She looked worried and confused at the same time. "What happened?"

"I— I—" Bridget stammered, unsure of what to say. "What are you guys doing at Ms. Diaz's house? Why didn't you tell me you two were dating? I thought we were friends!"

"Dating?" Emma asked, looking even more confused.

"Me and Emma? We're not dating!" Eric exclaimed, clearly annoyed. "Were you spying on us? Really?"

Bridget didn't quite believe them. "But then why are you hanging out here? And, you've both been acting super weird!"

Emma gave Eric a look, and he shrugged.

"I guess we'll just tell you now," Emma said, rolling her eyes.

"Tell me what?" Bridget demanded, putting her hands on her hips.

"Gosh, Gadget," Emma said, exasperated. "We're trying to do something *nice* for you. We knew you really wanted to go to that science fair and meet Dr. Knutson. So, we worked out a deal with Ms. Diaz to clean her garage for fifty bucks."

Bridget felt as if the air had been sucked right out of her lungs. She'd been so completely wrong.

"You did what?" she asked, shocked.

Eric chimed in, "We didn't tell you about it because we wanted it to be a surprise. We were going to finish cleaning the garage today and tell you tomorrow. We didn't know you'd . . . ya know . . . spy on us with the drone."

Bridget felt her face get red.

"You should've trusted us," Emma said finally. "Don't you think I'd tell you if I started dating someone?"

"Yeah, but . . ." Bridget didn't know what else to say. "I just worried that if you guys were dating, it'd change our friendship. I never guessed that you would be doing this amazing thing for me." Bridget sighed. "I'm so sorry."

Bridget barely had the words out of her mouth before she felt Emma giving her a big hug. Eric reached over and gave her a solid pat on the back.

"It's okay, Gadg," Eric said.

"Yeah," Emma said. "I'm sorry you were so worried. We never meant that, of course!"

"Are we really going to the Technology in Science Fair?" Bridget said. She still couldn't believe her friends had done this for her. "We're going to meet Margaret Knutson?"

"Sure, if you let us finish cleaning this garage!" Eric said, gesturing at the garage behind them.

Bridget hunched over the drone on the ground. "I want to help you guys with the garage, if you'll let me. But first, I've got to make sure this thing still works. If it doesn't, I'm in trouble. I don't know what I was thinking."

"It landed pretty softly," Emma noted.

Bridget picked up the drone and inspected it. The "on" button had switched to the "off" position during the drone's crash landing. Bridget flipped the switch. The drone came to life, and so did the controller app.

"Whew," Bridget breathed. "I think it's okay." Bridget successfully piloted the drone up into the air and landed it on the grass again.

"Man, you are lucky," Eric said.

"*Really* lucky," Bridget agreed.

Several weeks later, Bridget was sitting with Eric and Emma in the auditorium at Cyber Hills Technology Center, where the Technology in Science Fair was being held. They had already presented their project earlier in the day. Dr. Margaret Knutson was now taking the stage to announce the winners.

"Before I announce the winner and our runners-up," Dr. Knutson said from the podium, "I want to talk a little bit about responsibility and technology. The more new technology we are presented with, the more important it is for us to learn to use it responsibly. In my research with wolves in national parks, it was always my first goal to avoid disrupting the wolves. Nature deserves our respect. The misuse of technology can be harmful to the world around us."

Bridget understood exactly what Dr. Knutson was talking about. Although she and her friends had been careful not to disturb the foxes during their project, Bridget knew she'd been irresponsible when she used the drone to spy on her friends. Bridget felt like she didn't deserve to win the award.

"All of our finalists have demonstrated a respect for the natural world. I will first announce the runners-up."

Bridget's heart started to beat faster.

"Our first runner-up is Bridget Grant, Eric Miller, and Emma Hein for their work observing foxes in Cyber Hills."

Bridget practically leapt up the stairs to the stage. Dr. Knutson handed her a plaque and motioned that she should say something at the podium.

"Wow," Bridget breathed into the microphone, looking out at the crowd. While she didn't win the grand prize, she was excited to be standing next to one of her heroes.

"This is such an honor. I need to thank my research partners, Emma and Eric, as well as Lingo for allowing me to use one of their new silent drones. I think what Dr. Knutson said about respect is important. Not only is it important to respect your research subject, but also your research partners—your friends."

Bridget took a deep breath. "It's because of them that I'm standing here today. Thank you!"

Before Bridget could step off the stage, Dr. Knutson came over and shook her hand.

"Great work, Bridget," Dr. Knutson said, "You and your friends did an excellent job in showing how technology can be used to study nature. I hope it's something you continue to do."

Bridget smiled. "Thank you," she said.

The End

Think About It

1. Bridget suspects her friends Eric and Emma of secretly dating. If you were her, how would you have found out the truth? Would you have tried to be sneaky about it, or would you have done something differently?

2. Bridget asked her teacher Ms. Diaz for $50 to enter the Technology in Science Fair contest. Are there other ways she could have tried to get the money? What would you have done if you were in her shoes?

3. Read another Bridget Gadget story. Then compare how Bridget treats her friends Eric and Emma in each of the stories. In *Drone Detective*, she is suspicious of them. Is this different in the other story? Do you feel that Bridget is a good friend? Use examples to explain your answer.

Write About It

1. How do you feel about drones being used to observe wildlife? Start by listing all the pros, as in the positive reasons for using drones, and then the cons, or the negative reasons. Looking at your two lists, write an argument for or against their use.

2. Using all the information you learned about foxes from this book and including any information you may know about them, write a short report about foxes.

3. If you were given the assignment to observe something in nature, such as a plant, an animal, or the stars, what would you choose to do a project about? Write down everything you know about the subject that you would pick. Then explain why you are interested in it.

About the Author

Mari Kesselring is a writer and editor of books for young people. She's written on various subjects, including William Shakespeare, Franklin D. Roosevelt, and the attack on Pearl Harbor. She is currently pursuing a Master of Fine Arts in Creative Writing at Hamline University. Like Bridget, Mari enjoys technology and new gadgets. She appreciates how technology provides unlimited access to knowledge and brings people closer together. Mari lives in St. Paul, Minnesota, with her husband and their dog, Lady.

About the Illustrator

Mariano Epelbaum has illustrated books for publishers in the United States, Puerto Rico, Spain, and Argentina. He has also worked as an animator for commercials, television shows, and movies, such as *Pantriste*, *Micaela*, and *Manuelita*. Mariano was also the art director and character designer for *Underdogs*, an animated movie about foosball. He currently lives in Buenos Aires, Argentina.

More Fun with Bridget Gadget

Digital Reveal

Bridget secretly writes a review of TechPaper, a paper-thin tablet that her dad's company is developing. No one is supposed to know about the device yet. But that all changes when Bridget's post with pictures of the device goes viral.

Fitness Crash

Bridget feels pressured to get in better shape for soccer. So she gets a fitness gadget made by her dad's technology company to help her reach her fitness goals. Will she push herself too hard to get into better shape?

Pixel Perfection

Bridget and Emma are surprised by the attention they receive after the launch of their e-zine, *Cyber Hills Holler*. However, when they start editing photos of their classmates to retain their new-found popularity, not everyone is happy with the results.

READ MORE FROM 12-STORY LIBRARY

EVERY 12-STORY LIBRARY BOOK IS AVAILABLE IN MANY FORMATS, INCLUDING AMAZON KINDLE AND APPLE IBOOKS. FOR MORE INFORMATION, VISIT YOUR DEVICE'S STORE OR 12STORYLIBRARY.COM.